[redacted]

The Shoemaker
and the Elves

ILLUSTRATED BY ADRIENNE ADAMS

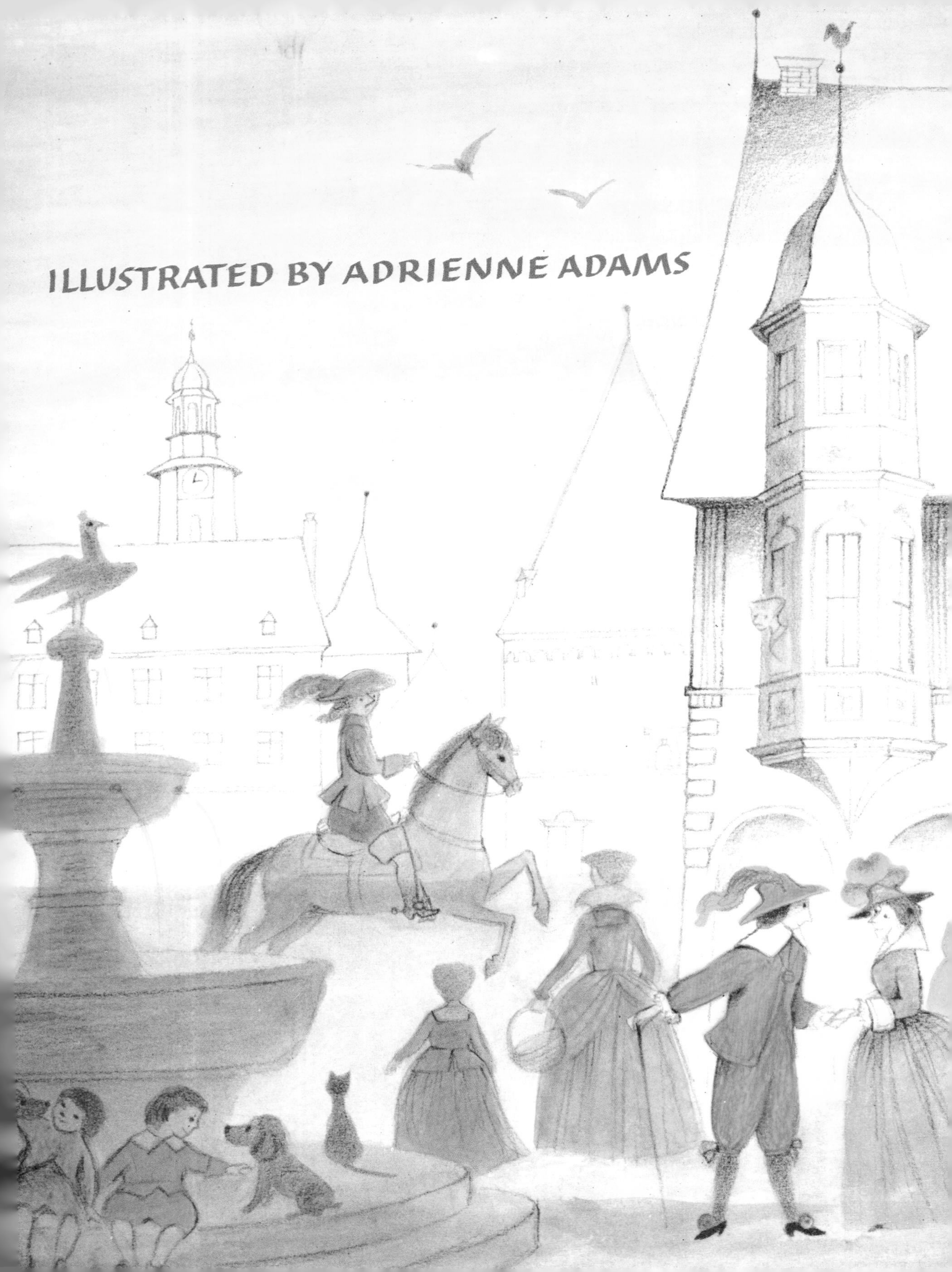

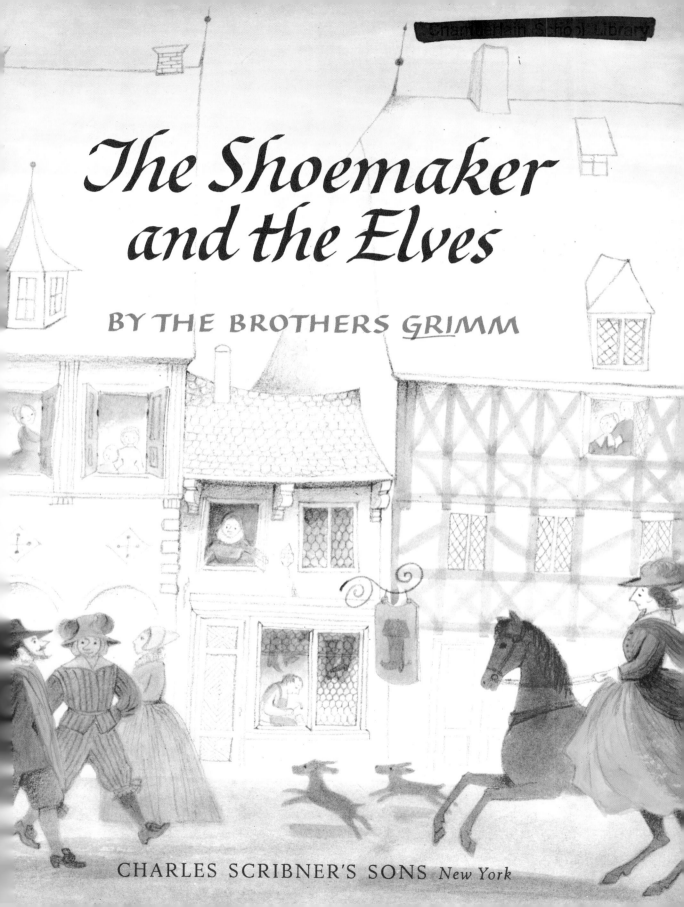

The Shoemaker and the Elves

BY THE BROTHERS GRIMM

CHARLES SCRIBNER'S SONS *New York*

Translation by Wayne Andrews

Pictures copyright © 1960 by Adrienne Adams
Translation copyright © 1960 by Charles Scribner's Sons

Charles Scribner's Sons
Macmillan Publishing Company
866 Third Avenue, New York, NY 10022
Collier Macmillan Canada, Inc.

Printed in the United States of America

First Edition

15 17 19 21 23 25 RH/C 24 22 20 18 16 14

Library of Congress Card Catalog Number 60-12607
ISBN 0-684-12982-5

For Suzy Farren

There once was a shoemaker who had become so poor through no fault of his own that he had nothing left in the world but the leather to make a single pair of shoes.

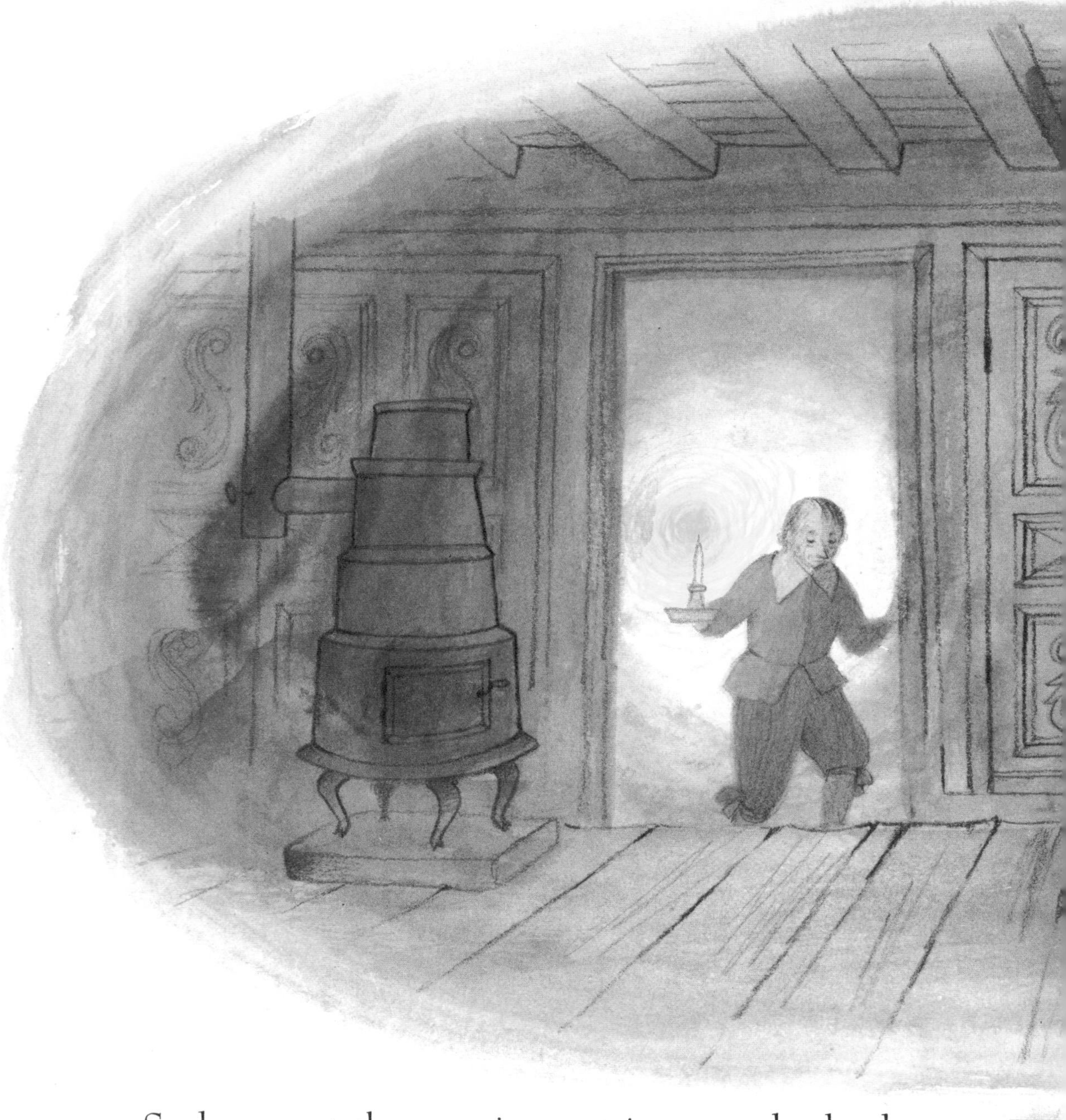

So he spent the evening cutting out the leather for the shoes he planned to make the next day.

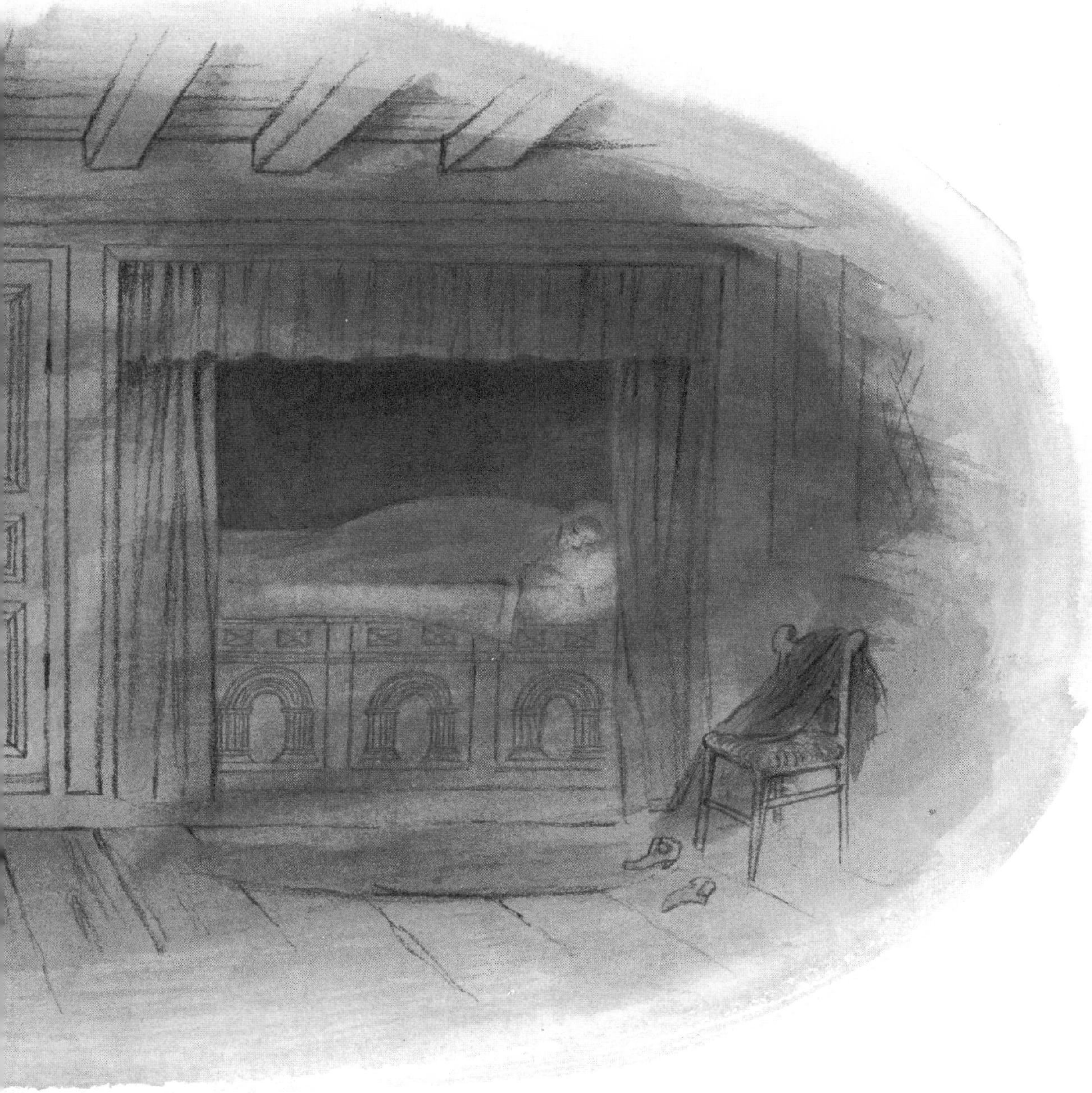

As he was at peace with the world, he lay down quietly on his bed and asked God's blessing. Then he went to sleep.

The next morning, after he had said
his prayers, and was about to get to work,
there stood the shoes on his table,
completely finished. He was surprised and
did not know what to make of this. He took the
shoes in his hands, and looked at them closely.
They were so well made that not a stitch was
missing, just as if a master shoemaker had been
at work.

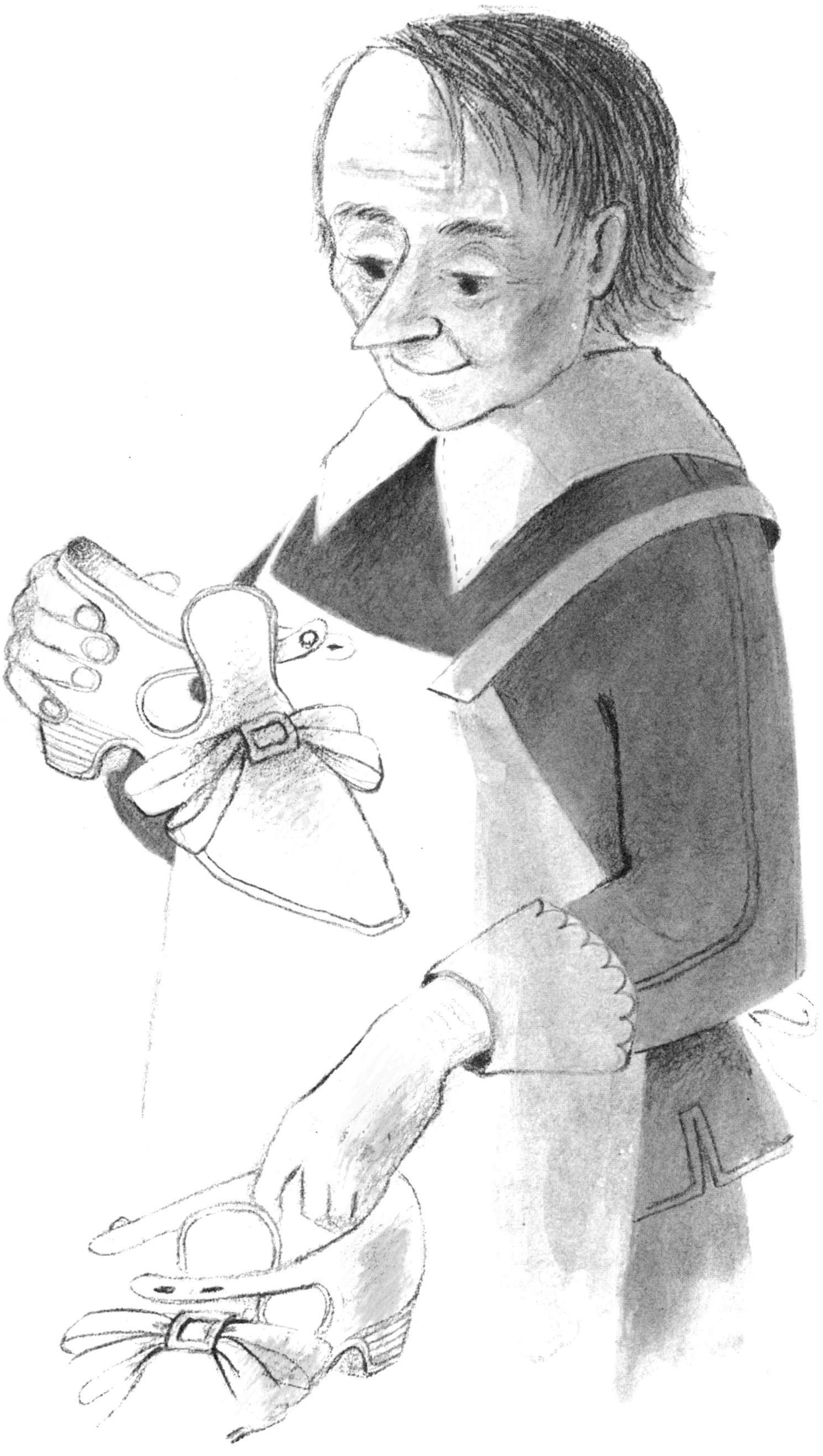

Right then and there a customer came in, and the shoes pleased him so well that he paid more than the usual price for them.

With the money he received, the shoemaker
was able to buy leather for two more pairs.
He cut them out in the evening

and the next morning was ready to set to work in high spirits. But he did not have to do any work, for when he got up there were the shoes, already finished.

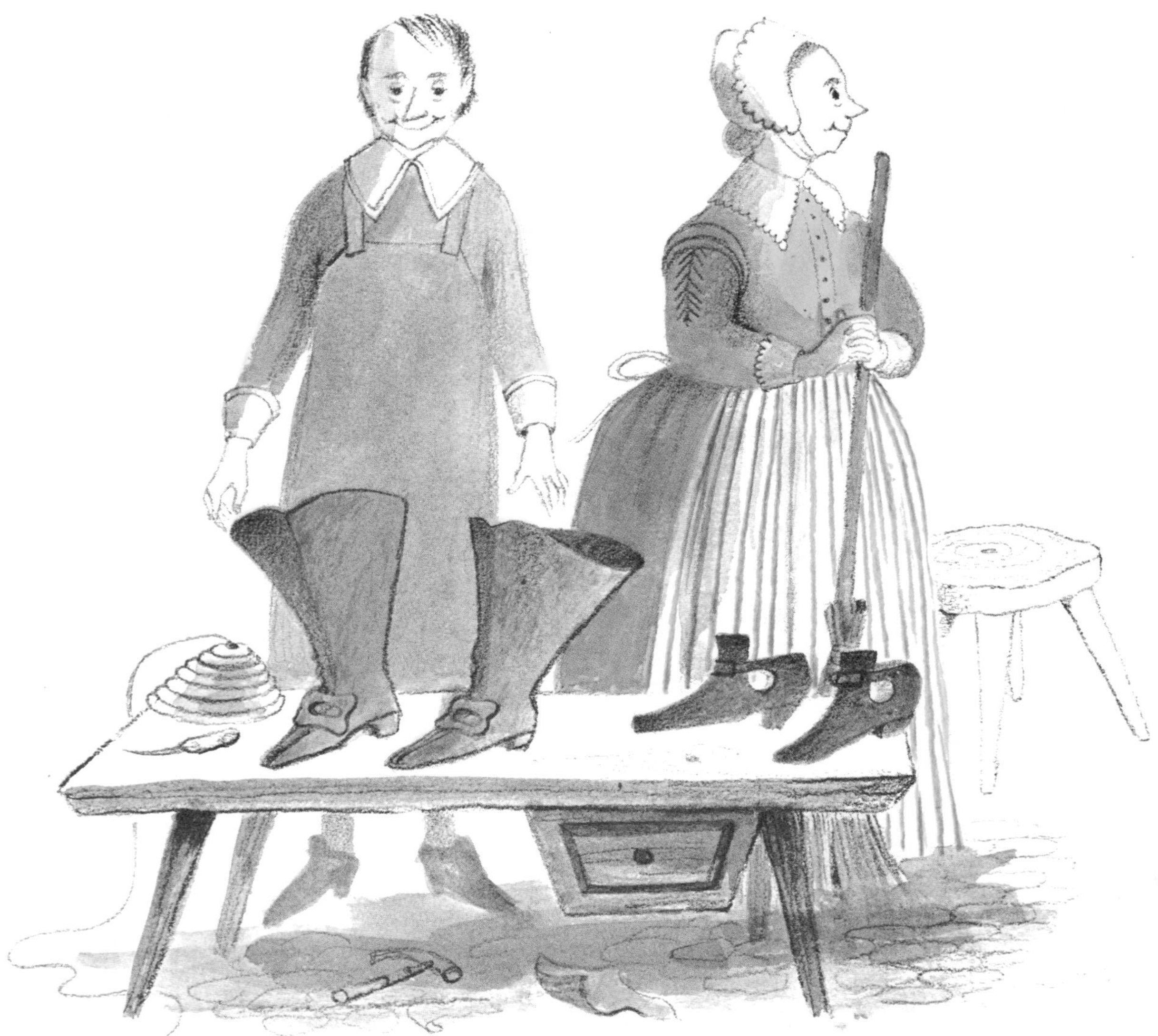

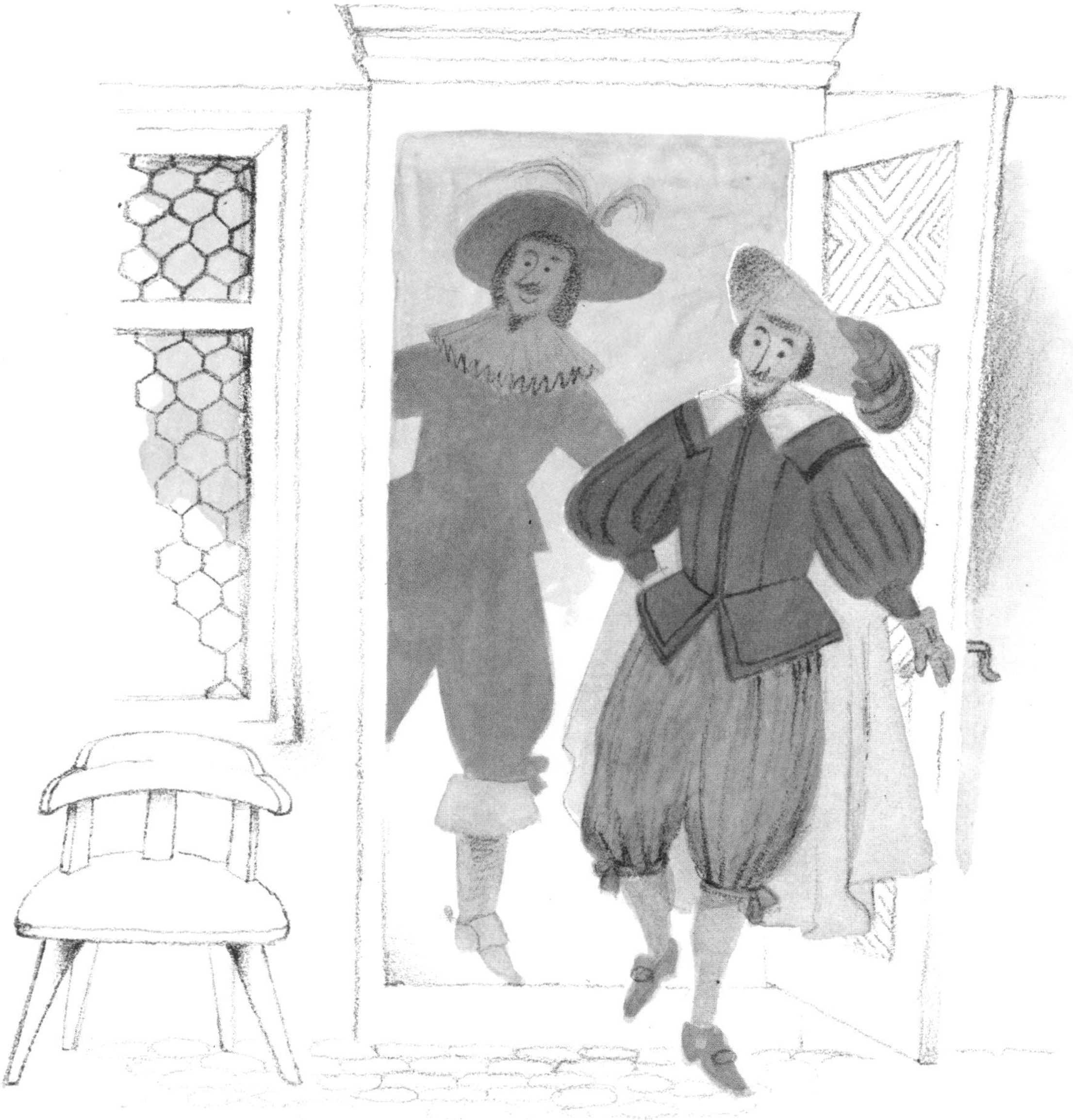

Customers came in and paid him such good prices that he was able to buy the leather for four pairs of shoes.

Early the next morning he found the four
pairs of shoes ready, too. And so it went,
on and on. Whatever leather he cut out in the
evening was made into shoes by the next
morning, so he was soon earning a good income
again and finally became a well-to-do man.

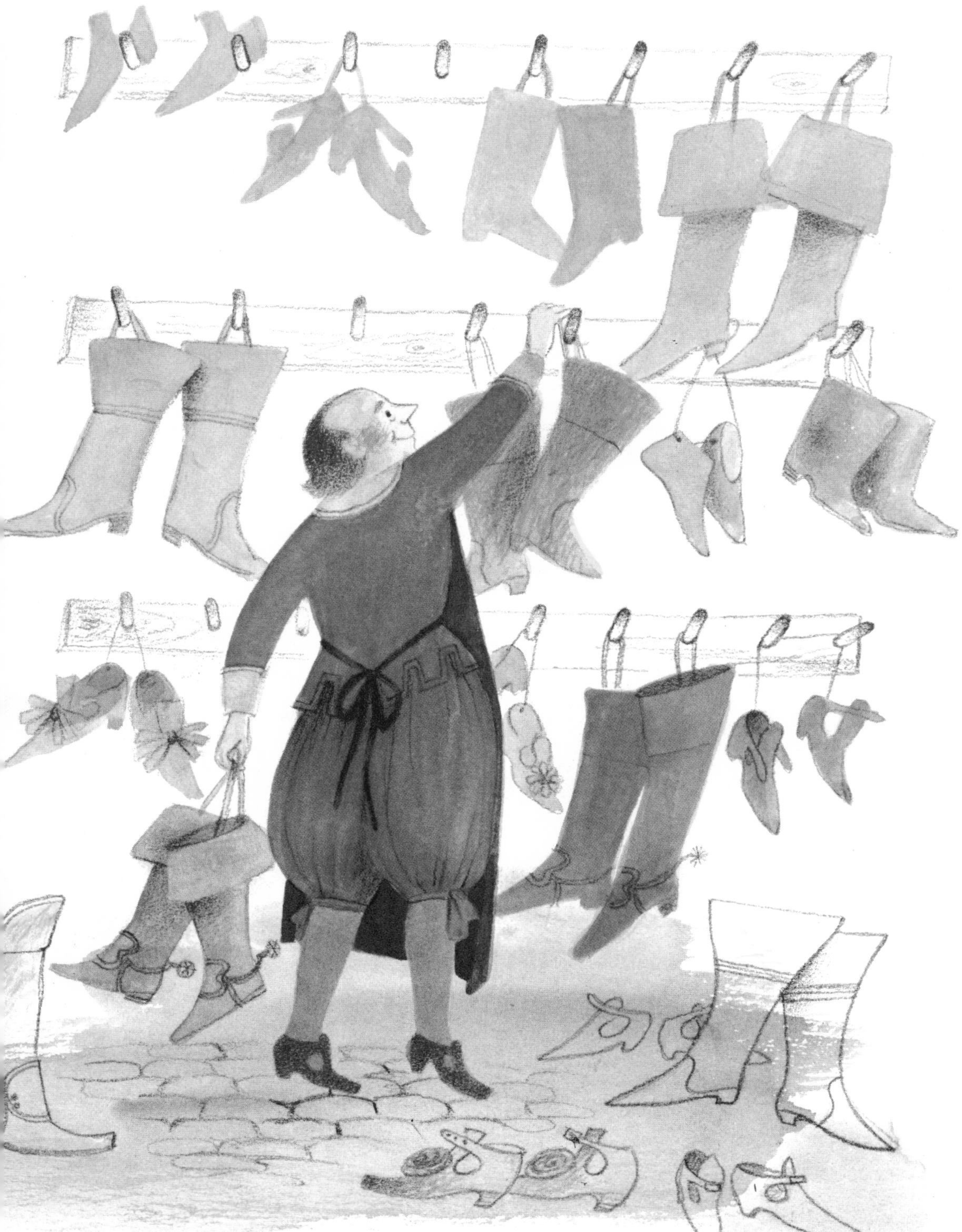

Now one evening not long before Christmas, after the man had cut out the leather once more, he said to his wife before he went to bed: "How would it be if we stayed up tonight and found out just who is lending us such a helping hand?" His wife thought this was a good idea, and lighted a candle. Then they hid in a corner of the room, behind all the clothes that were hung up there, and kept their eyes open.

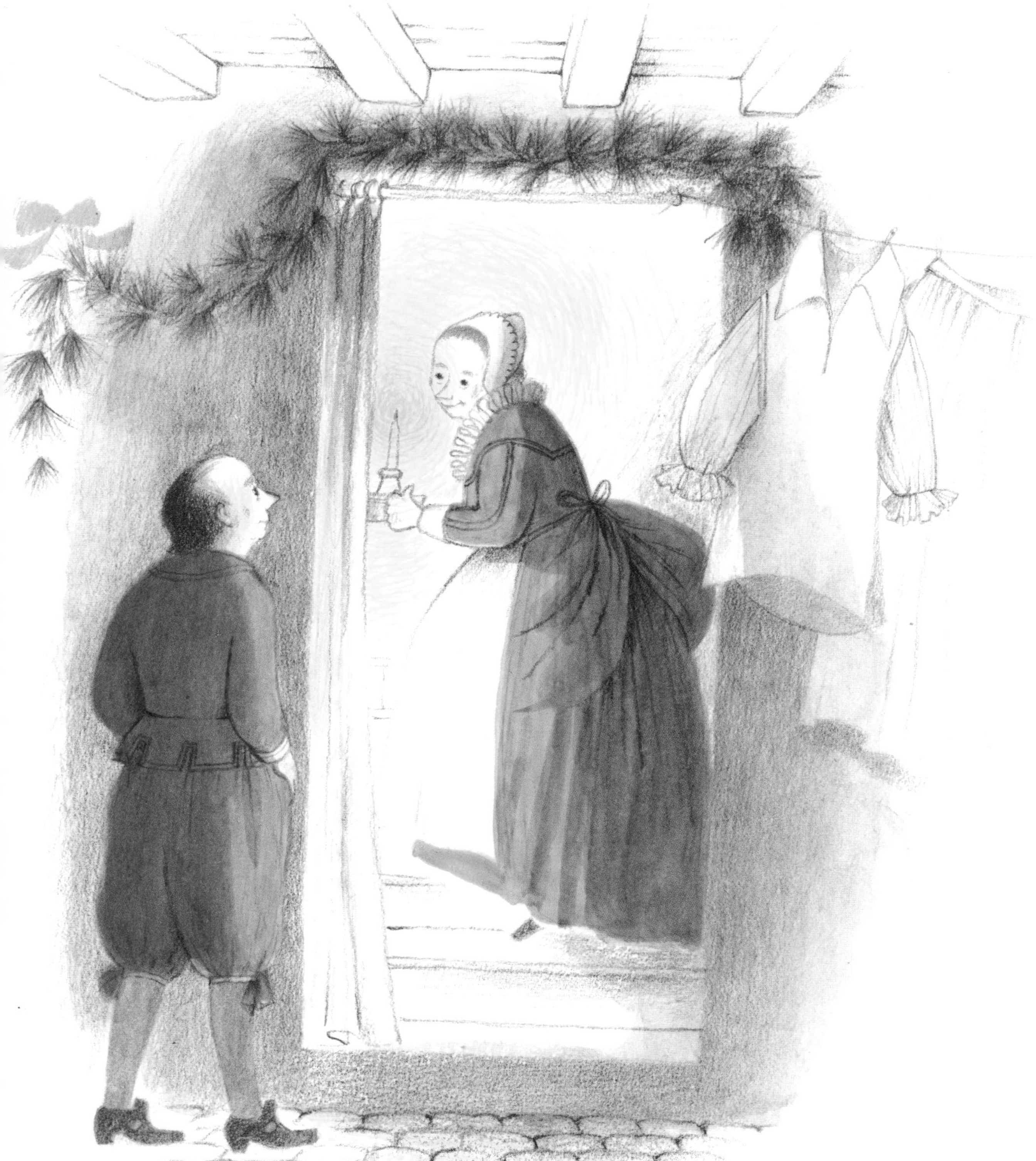

At the stroke of midnight in came two little men who had no clothes on. They sat down at the shoe-maker's table and took all the work that had been laid out for them. With their tiny fingers they began to stitch, sew and hammer so quickly and so nimbly, that the shoemaker was surprised and could not keep his eyes off them. They kept right on until all the work was done and stood ready on the table. Then they darted out of the room.

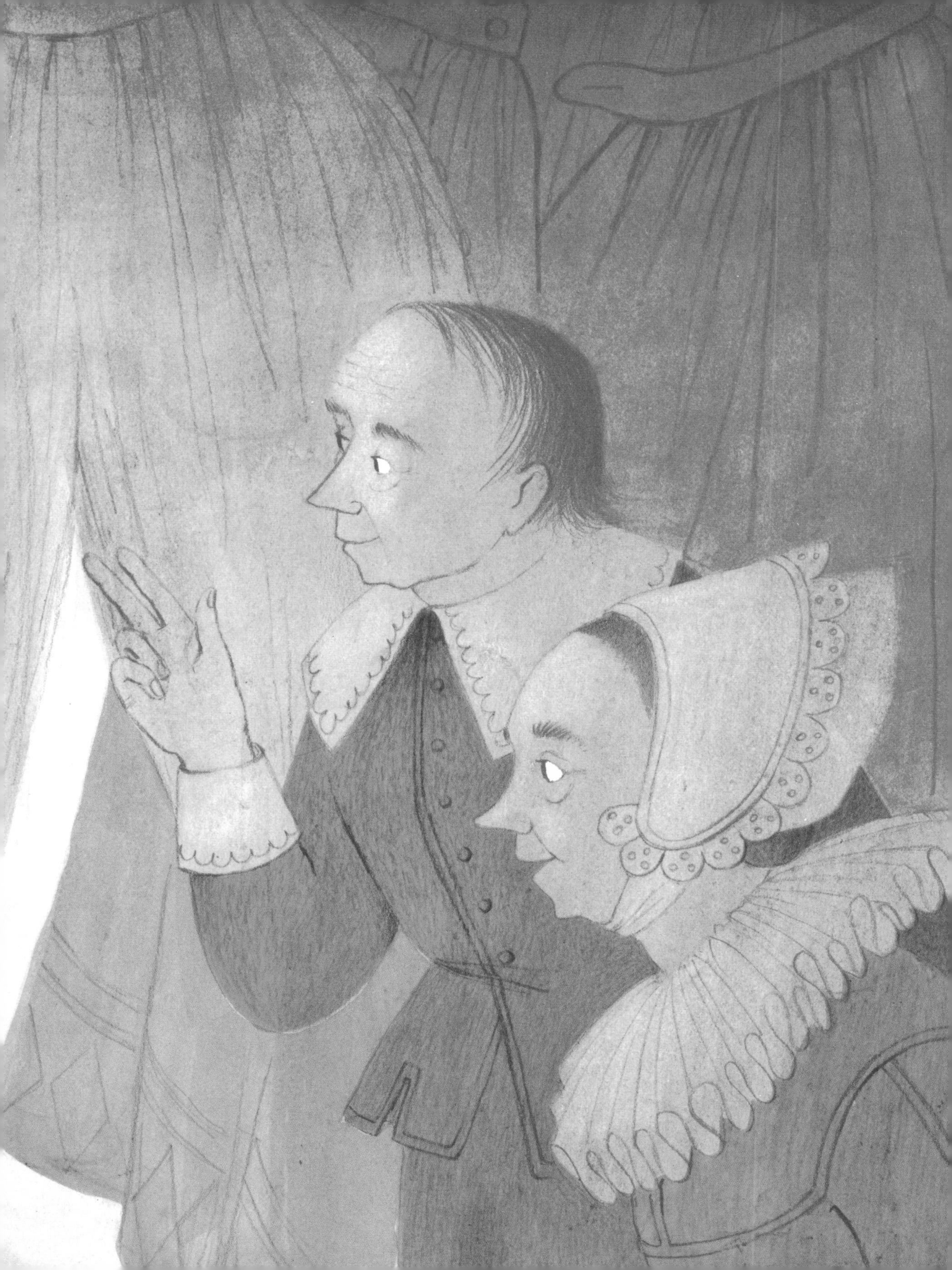

The next morning the shoemaker's wife said:
"The little men have made us rich. We must
show them that we are thankful. Here they are,
running around everywhere without a stitch on,
and they must be freezing. Do you know what?
I am going to sew little shirts, and coats,
and vests, and breeches for them, and knit a
pair of stockings for each of them, and you must
make a pair of shoes for each of them, too."
Her husband said: "I'll be very happy to do that."

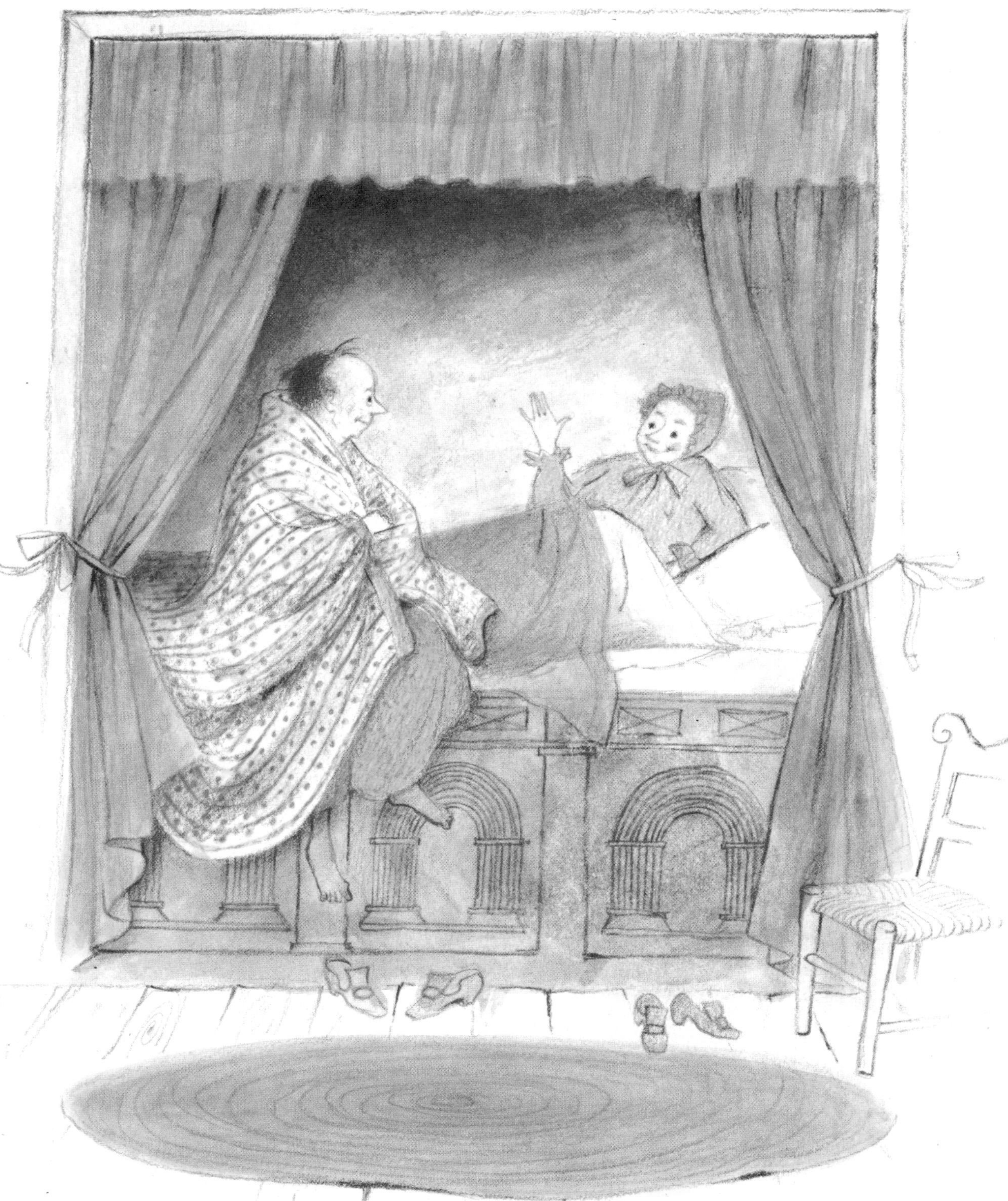

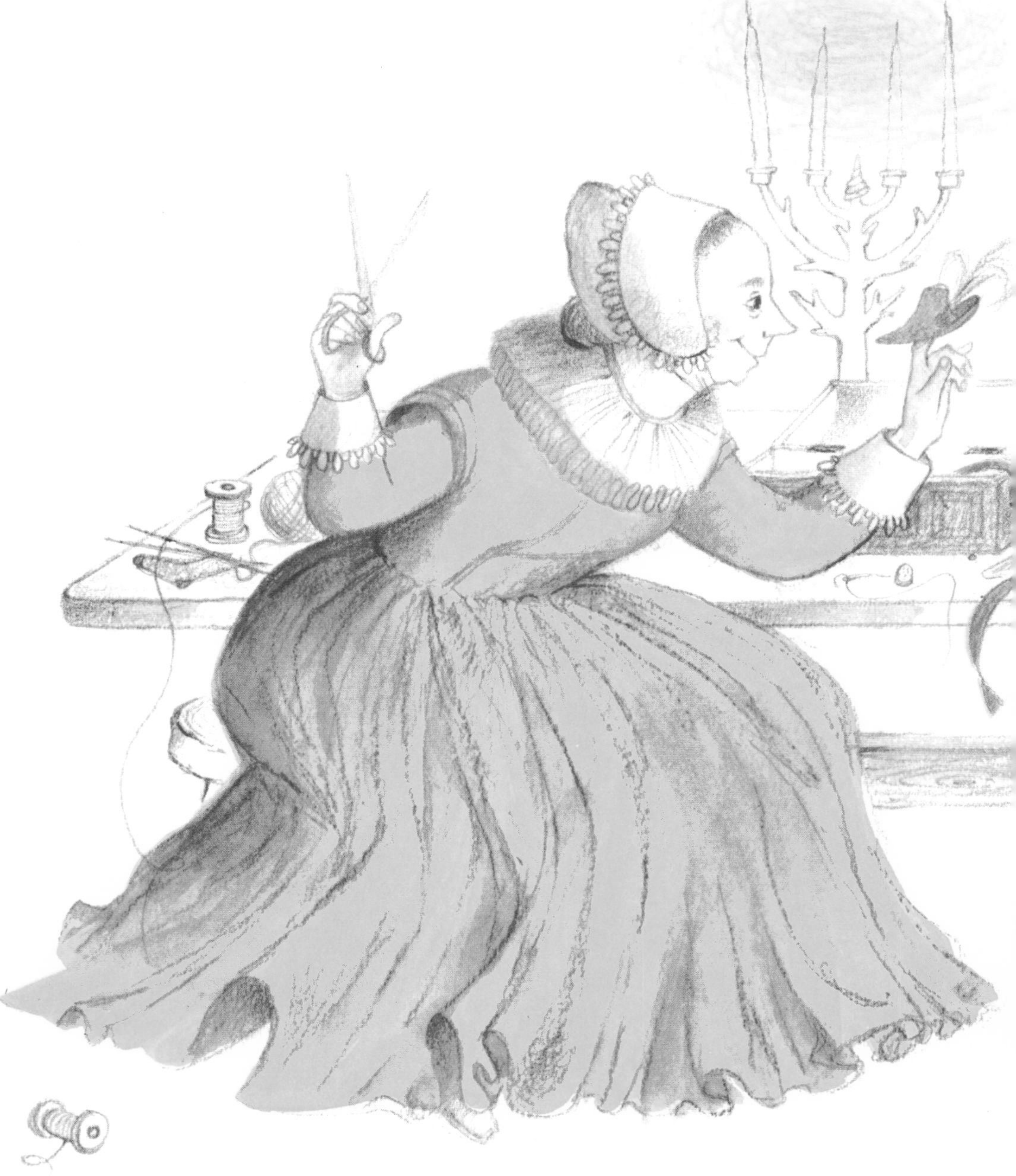

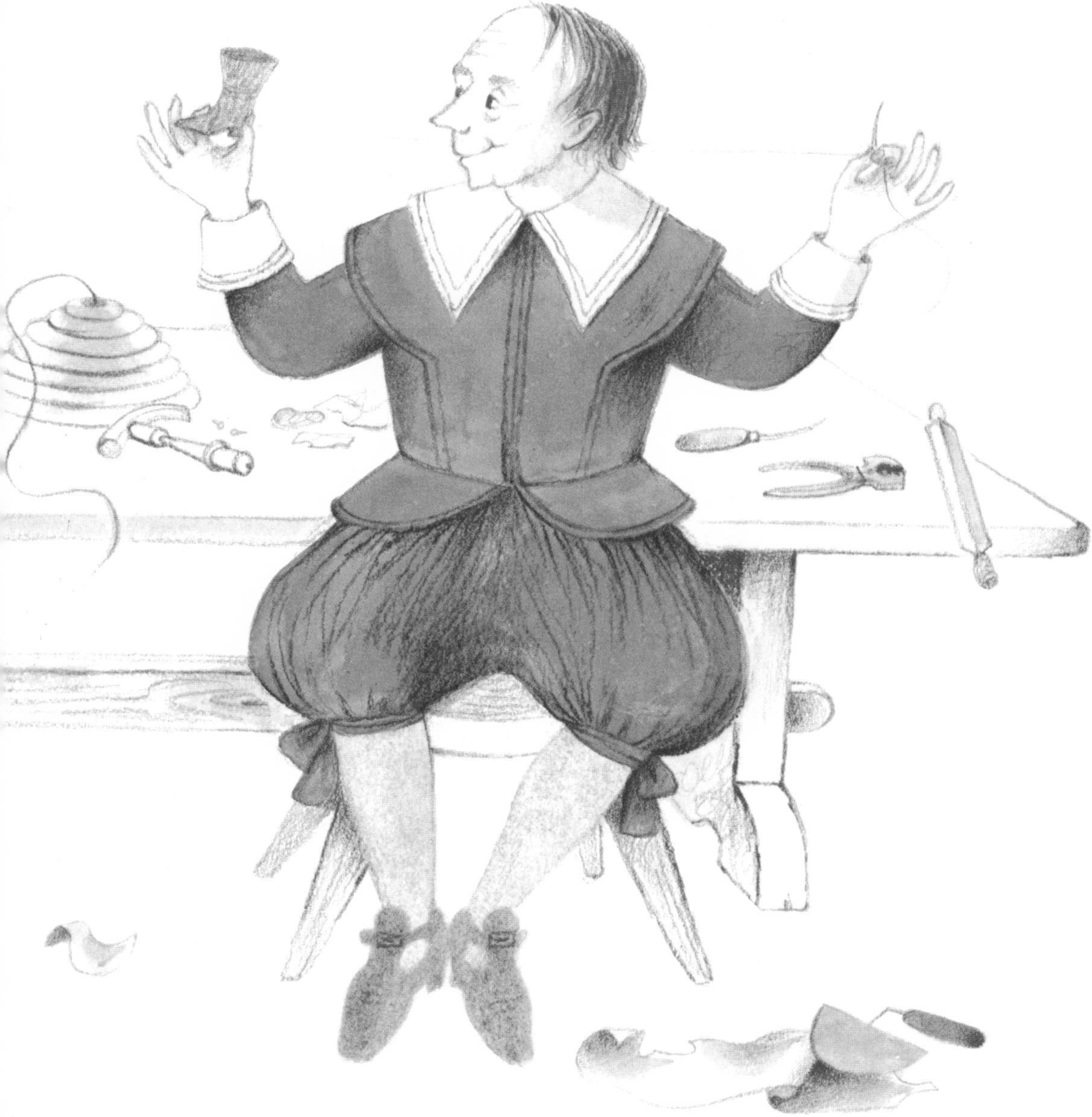

And in the evening, when they had everything ready, they laid their presents on the table instead of the work that had been cut out. Then they hid to see how the little men would behave. At midnight they came dancing in, and were all ready to set to work. When they found there was no leather cut out for them, but the pretty clothes, they were first of all surprised. Then they showed how happy they were.

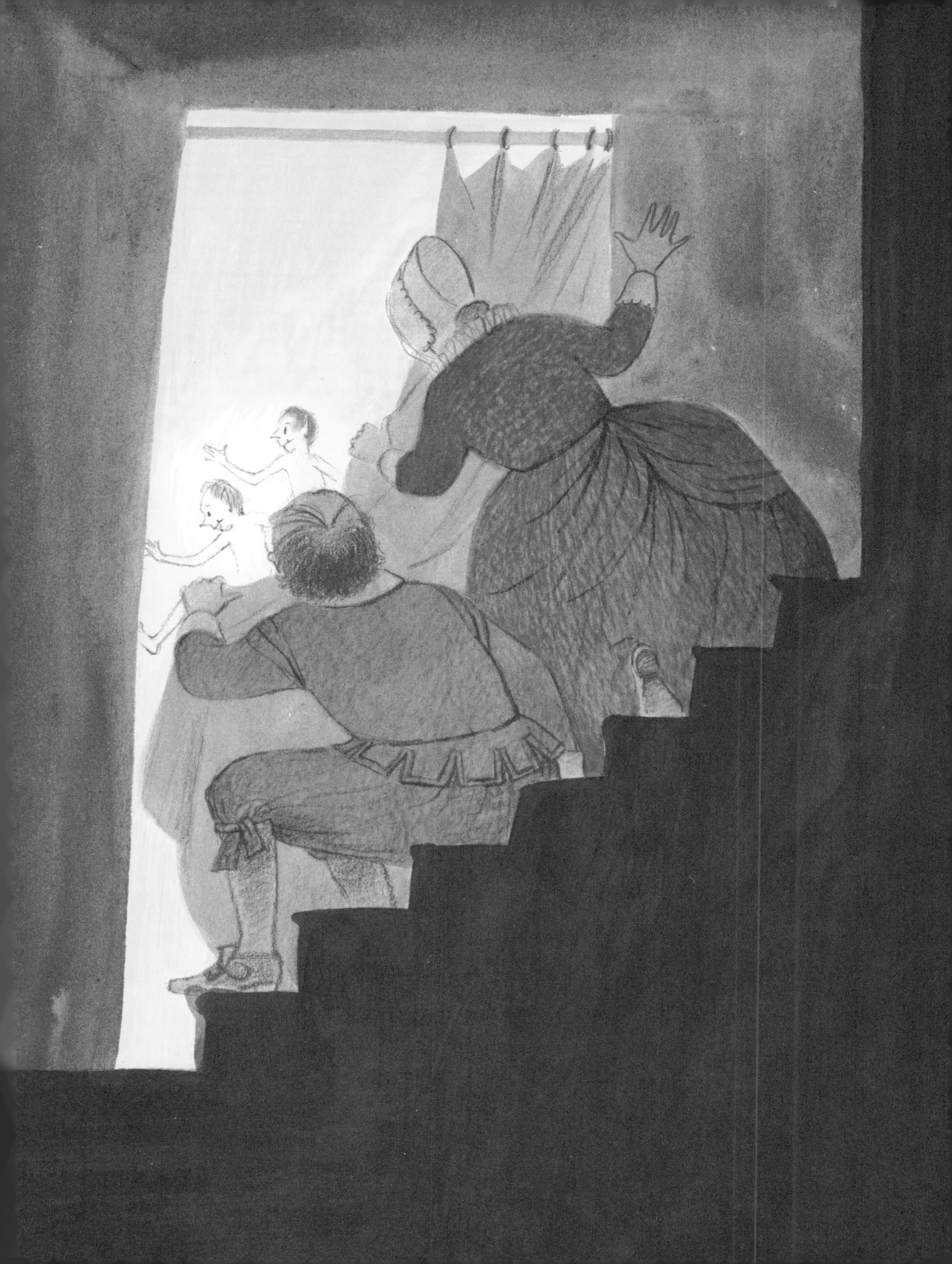

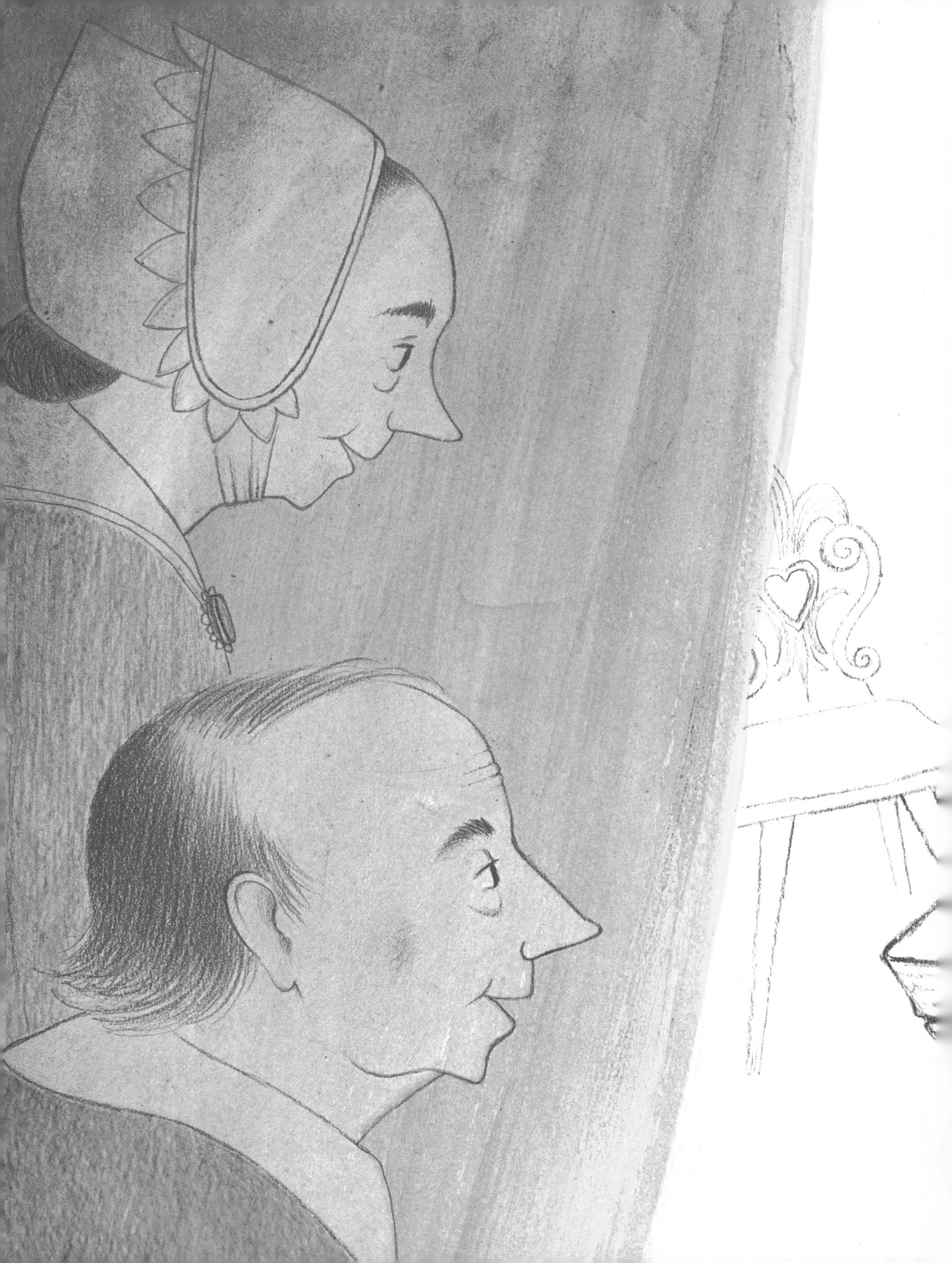

As quick as could be, they dressed themselves up in their beautiful clothes, and sang out:

"Now we're boys so fine to see
No longer cobblers will we be!"

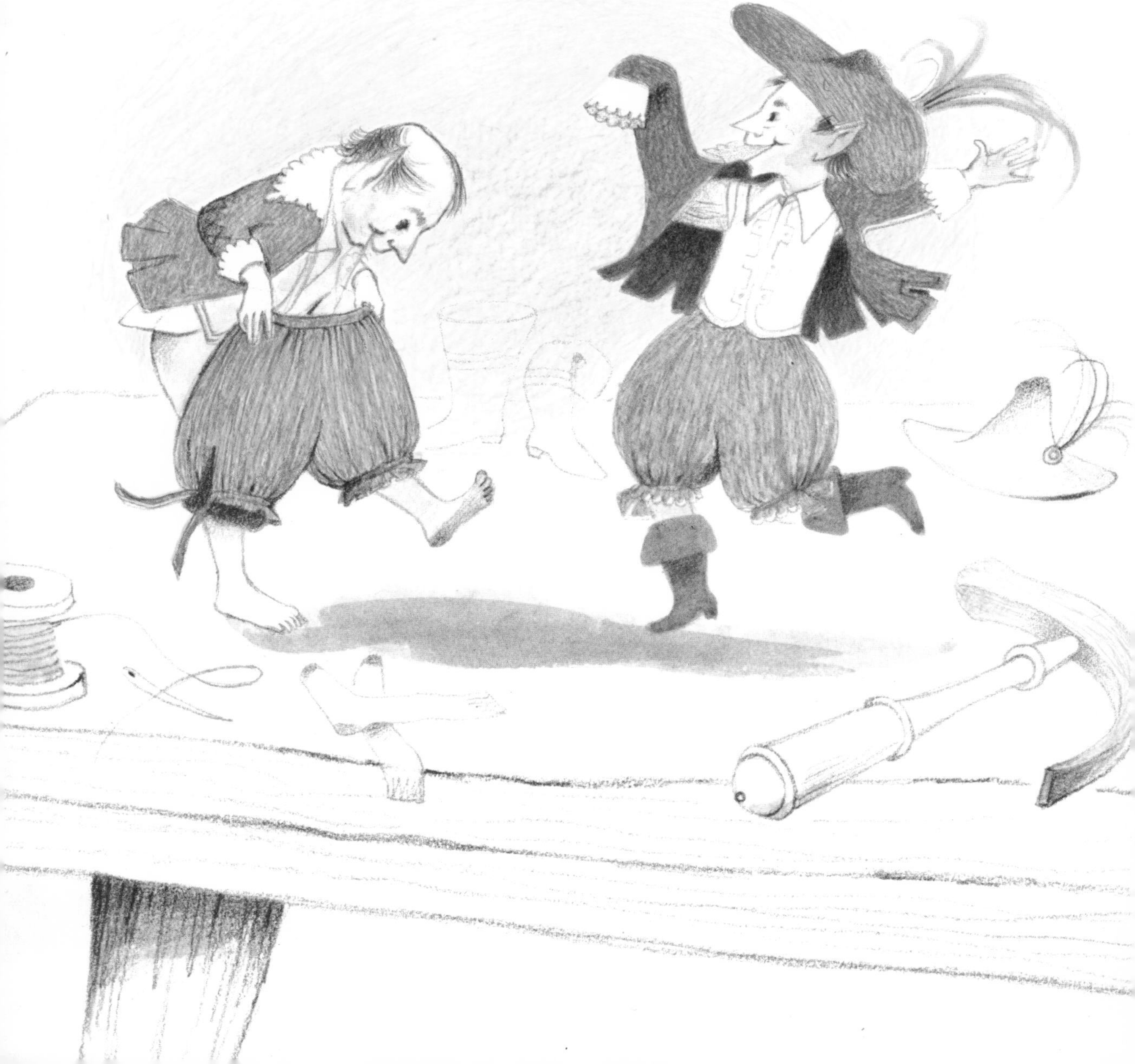

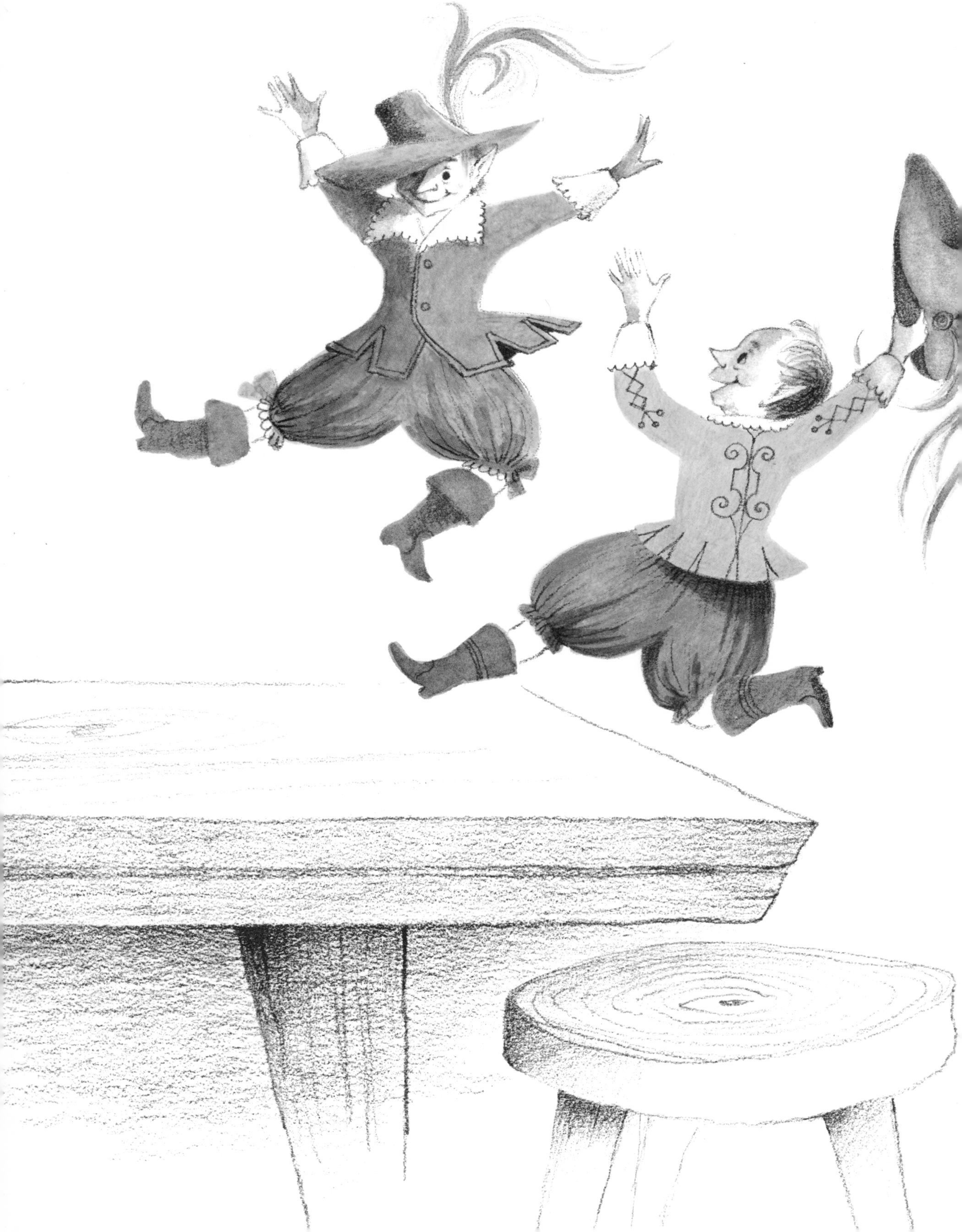

Then they hopped and they danced and they leaped over tables and chairs. Finally they danced out of the door.

From that time on they never came back, but everything went well with the shoemaker as long as he lived, and he was successful in everything he tried to do.

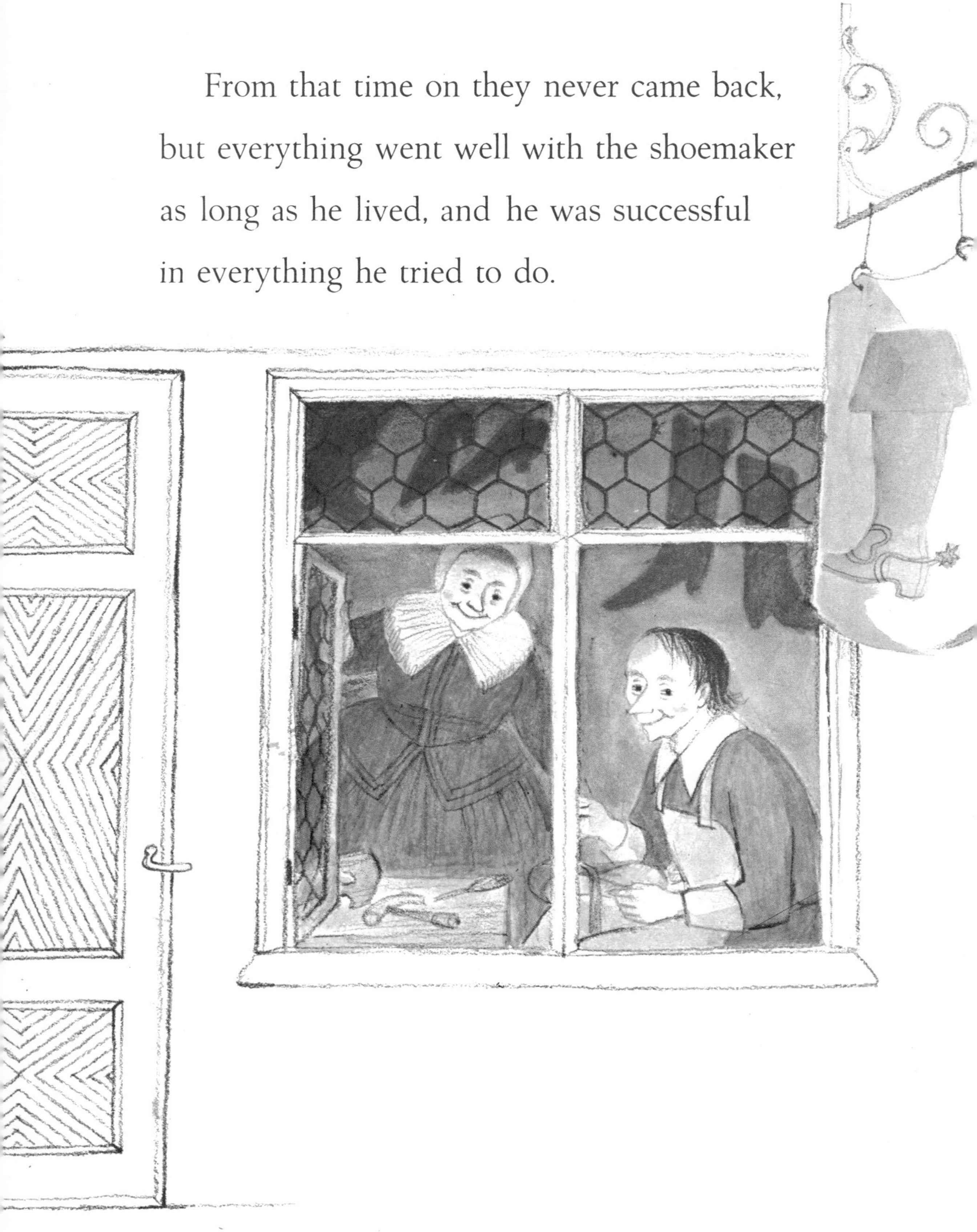